Electronic ACCESS

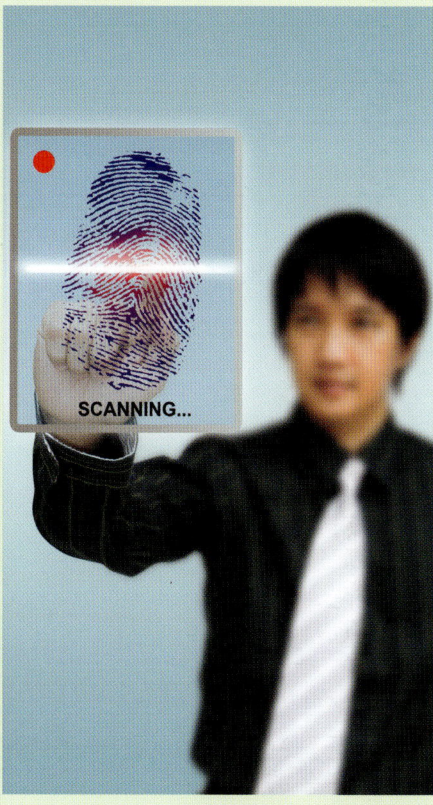

My sincere thanks to the following people for their time, information, images and enthusiasm for this book:

CSIRO, Canberra, Australia

Jennifer Sandercock, San Francisco, the USA

NBN Co., Sydney, Australia

Dear Reader

Just for a moment, think about times when you haven't been able to access the internet, or your mobile phone, or an app to play a game. On those occasions, we are reminded of just how much we rely on all forms of electronic access every day.

> **"I THOUGHT OF THE CHOCOLATE VENDING MACHINE WHERE MONEY WAS PUT IN A SLOT AND A BAR DISPATCHED. SURELY MONEY COULD BE DISPENSED IN THE SAME WAY."**
>
> JOHN SHEPHERD-BARRON
> INVENTOR OF ATM TECHNOLOGY

This book traces the history of access from metal keys and latches to many examples of electronic access. On pages 10–11, I am particularly delighted to feature the inventors of wi-fi technology – five Australian scientists.

Finally, in Chapter 11, meet Australian Jennifer Sandercock whose job it is to play games every day, so that she's inspired to design entertaining new computer games.

Enjoy!

Sharon Parsons

NELSON
CENGAGE Learning™
For learning solutions, visit **cengage.com.au**

Contents

Electronic ACCESS

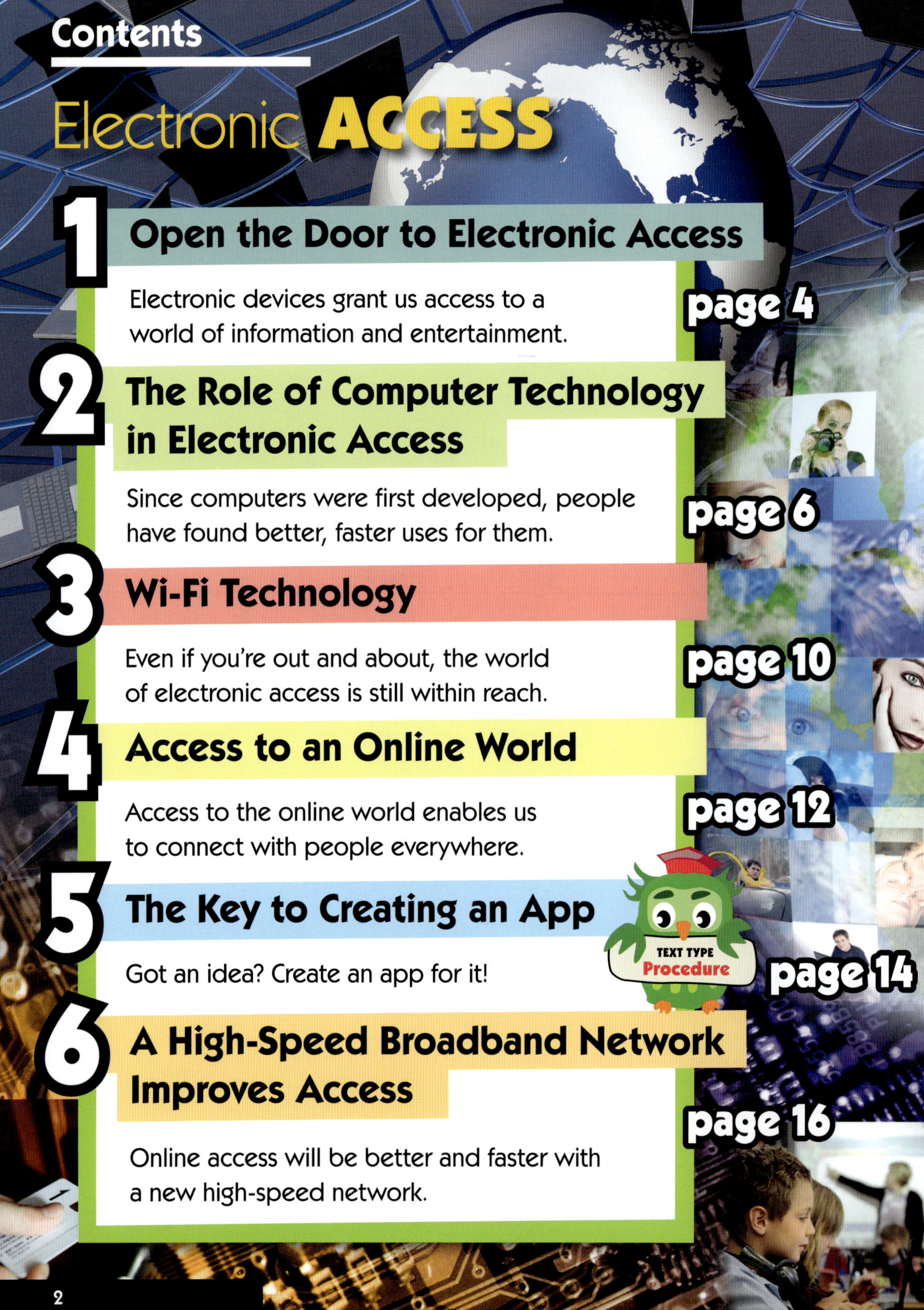

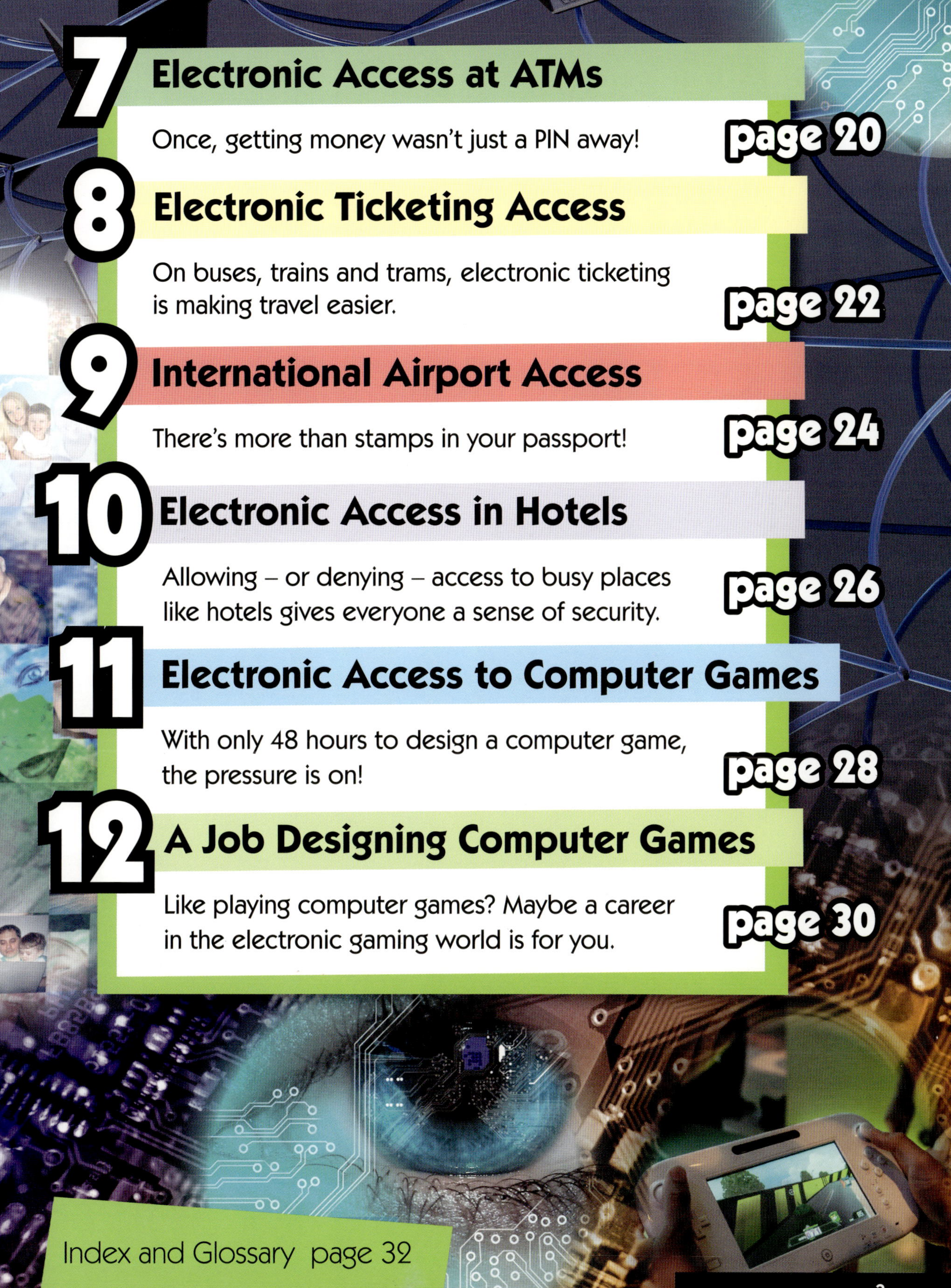

1 Open the Door to Electronic Access

For thousands of years, humans have invented ways of securing, limiting and monitoring access to their homes, workplaces, possessions, information, borders and roads. The evolution of devices that control access – from wooden door latches, to metal bolts and keys, to wireless electronic entry systems – shows how far humans will go to protect what's important to them.

Access in Earlier Times:
Latches

Manual Access:
Locks and keys

Typical Jobs:
Blacksmith
Carpenter
Locksmith

A PADLOCK INVENTOR

In 1921, American Harry Soref founded Master Lock, and in 1924 he and his team invented the world's first laminated steel padlock. Prior to this, padlocks were not sturdy enough and were easily destroyed.

a 1924 advertisment for laminated Master Lock padlocks (left)

Access in Recent Times:
Locks and keys

Electronic Access:
Locks and key cards

Wireless Electronic Access:
Unlock wirelessly

Typical Jobs:
Computer technician
Locksmith
Electrician

2 The Role of Computer Technology in Electronic Access

The pioneering period for computer inventions began in the 1940s, when computers were large, basic and operated very slowly compared to the technology we use today. Though these computers would not seem impressive today, at the time they were incredibly innovative, as the people who built them had only limited knowledge and resources to work with.

Almost 80 years later, this early work has set the foundation for the global technological community to improve computer design, write advanced software programs and design electronic devices that revolutionise how society works and communicates.

Computers Before the Internet: 1940s–1980s

1940s: First Commercial Computer

IBM, short for International Business Machines, is a United States company with a long history of technological invention stretching back as far as the 1890s.

1944: IBM invented the first computer to perform long calculations automatically.

1950s: Mainframe Computers

During this period, only governments and large organisations could afford the limited range of huge and very expensive computers.

1959: IBM invented its first mainframe computer, which could perform 229 000 calculations per second!

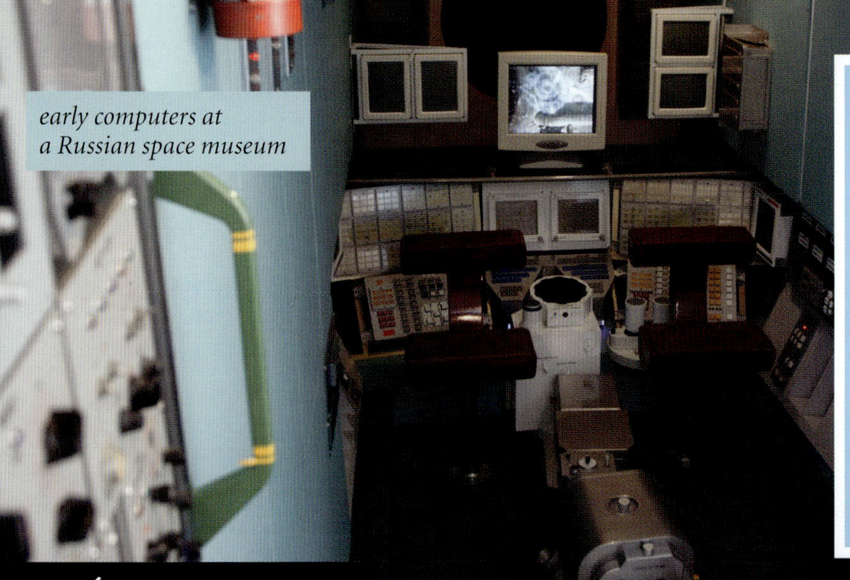

early computers at a Russian space museum

1960s: Space Computers

The use of computers for space exploration by the USSR and the USA led to significant results that culminated in the moon landing in 1969.

1969: Two *Apollo 11* astronauts became the first humans to land on the moon on 20 July 1969.

1970s: Personal Computers

This decade marked the rise in popularity of the personal computer.

1971: Intel Corporation engineers invented the first microprocessing chip. In 1974, a small firm called MITS made the first personal computer, the Altair, using Intel Corporation's 8080 microprocessor.

an early microprocessing chip (above)

1977: Apple II, a personal computer that was affordable for homes, small businesses and schools, was released.

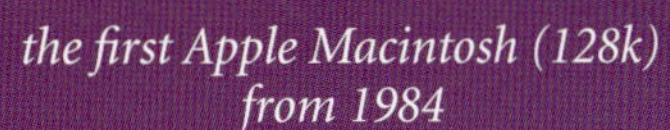

the first Apple Macintosh (128k) from 1984

APPLE FOUNDERS

Steve Jobs (1955–2011) and Stephen Wozniak (1959–) founded the Apple Company in 1976, California, USA.

Steve Jobs (left)

1980s: Personal Computers and Games

In the 1980s, video games became very popular.

1982: Compact discs became available.

1983: The first Nintendo gaming consoles were launched in Japan.

1989: Apple released its first portable Macintosh personal computer.

THEN

a Nintendo entertainment system with controllers

NOW

playing with a Nintendo WiiU controller at a world video games expo in 2012, Los Angeles, USA

Computers Since the Internet: 1990s–Present

Welcome to the internet!

inventor and founder of the World Wide Web Sir Tim Berners-Lee making a presentation in 2012

1990s: Internet-Fuelled Electronic Access

In 1989, British computer scientist Sir Tim Berners-Lee developed software that allowed people to share information on the internet. By the following year, the World Wide Web was available and this technology inspired companies to create products that made use of the new global information networks, such as laptops and downloadable entertainment.

1990: Internet access became available.

1995: Microsoft launched Internet Explorer.

1995: DVDs were introduced to the market.

a DVD player

1996: 3D graphics enabled more advanced computer games.

1996: Hotmail email accounts became popular.

an Apple iPhone 3GS, the third generation smartphone, released in 2009 (the original iPhone 3 was produced in 2007)

2000s: Millions More Access an Online World

By the year 2000, almost 400 million people had become connected to the internet and billions of emails were being sent, outstripping the volume of postal mail.

2001: Portable media players became popular.

2007: Smartphones appeared on the market.

2010s: Online Everywhere!

New generations of personal computing devices continue to fill the market. Many competing hardware and software companies design similar devices to offer consumers choice of products for all kinds of uses, such as apps and games.

2010: Touch-screen tablet computers became available.

3 Wi-Fi Technology

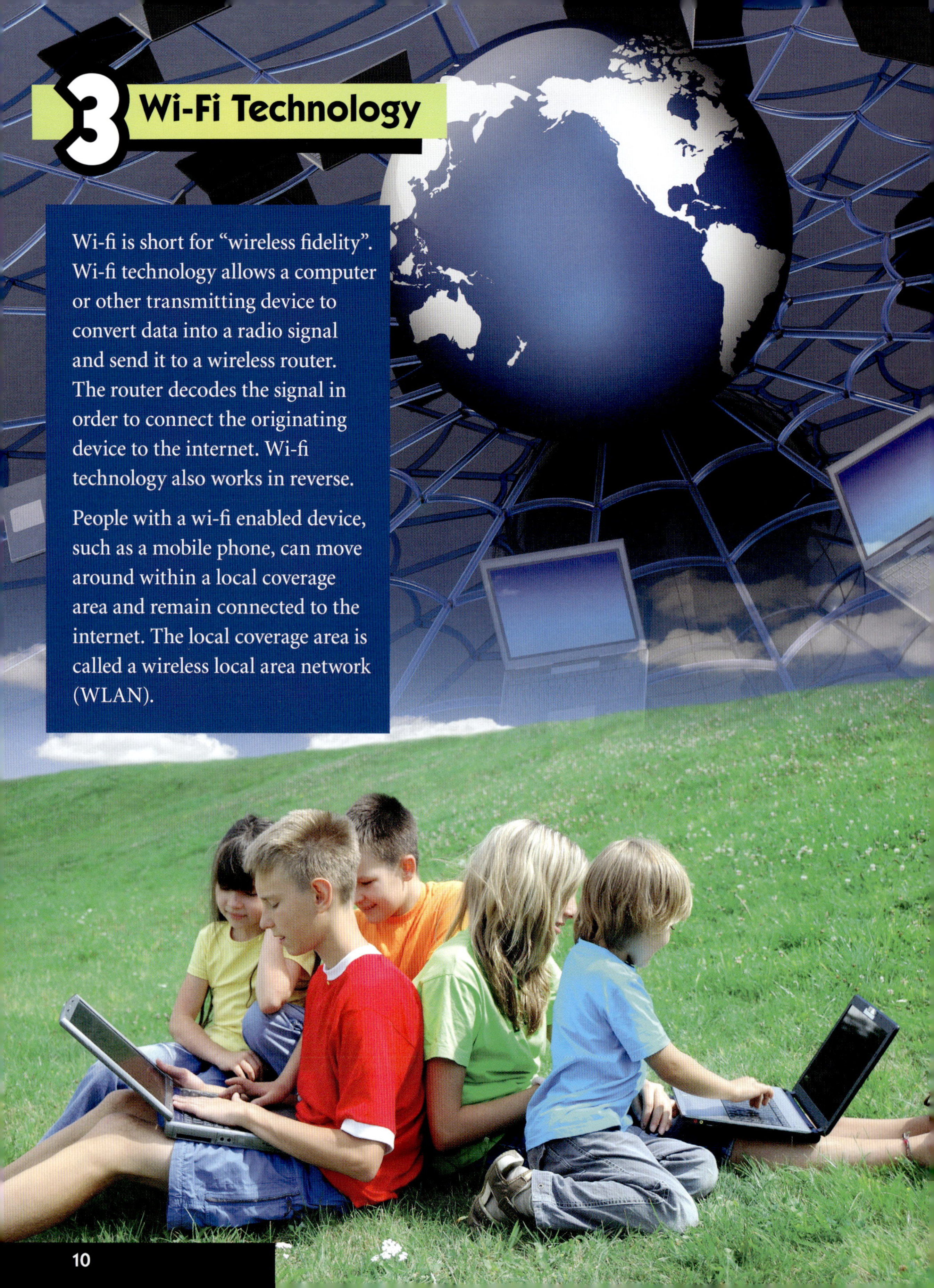

Wi-fi is short for "wireless fidelity". Wi-fi technology allows a computer or other transmitting device to convert data into a radio signal and send it to a wireless router. The router decodes the signal in order to connect the originating device to the internet. Wi-fi technology also works in reverse.

People with a wi-fi enabled device, such as a mobile phone, can move around within a local coverage area and remain connected to the internet. The local coverage area is called a wireless local area network (WLAN).

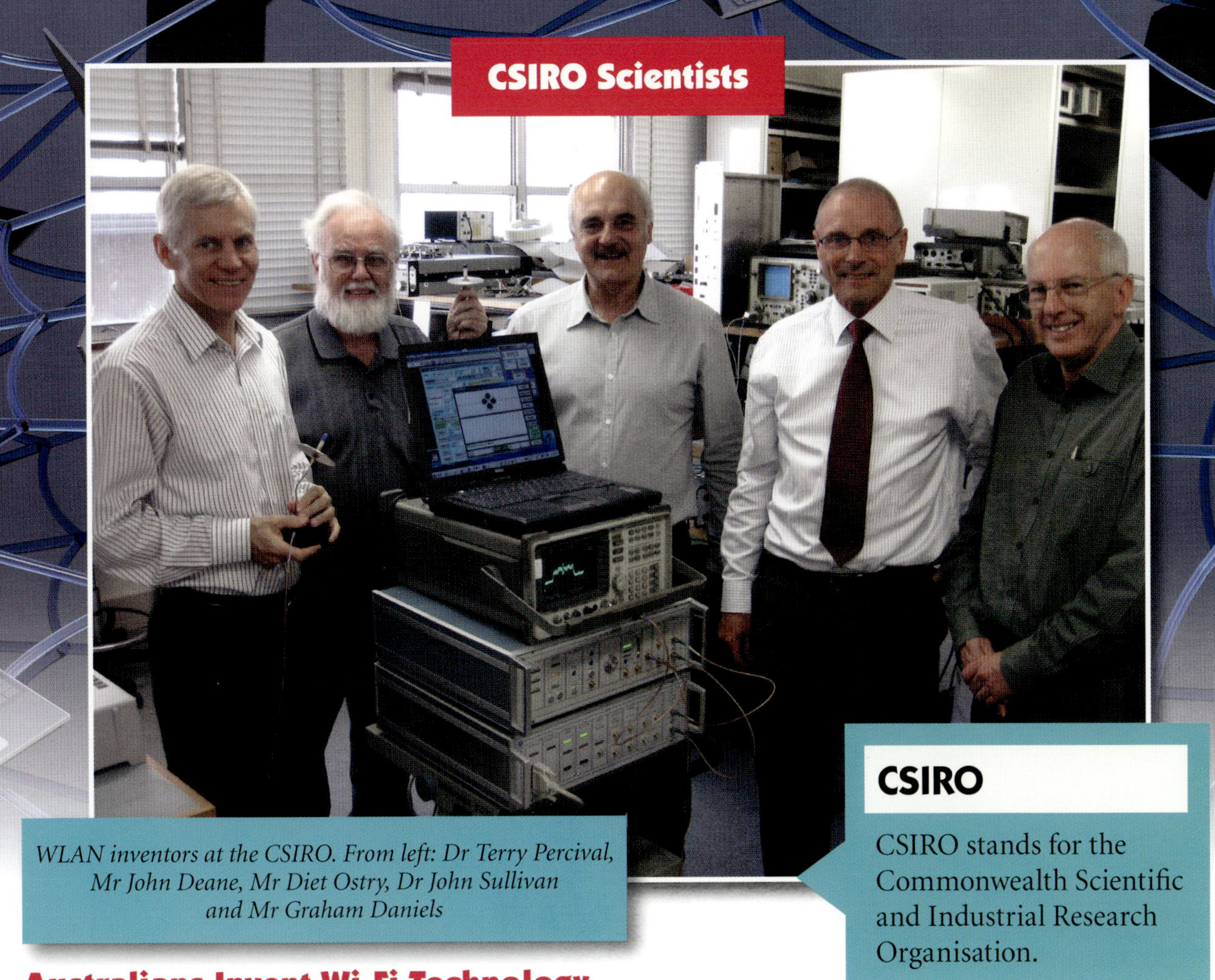

WLAN inventors at the CSIRO. From left: Dr Terry Percival, Mr John Deane, Mr Diet Ostry, Dr John Sullivan and Mr Graham Daniels

CSIRO

CSIRO stands for the Commonwealth Scientific and Industrial Research Organisation.

Australians Invent Wi-Fi Technology

When next you access a wi-fi hotspot at home or school, think about the team of Australian CSIRO scientists who invented the core technology for WLAN, which became the basis for wi-fi. This technology was patented in 1996. Fast WLAN technology is estimated to be in over five billion devices, such as computers, printers, mobile phones and televisions, worldwide.

How Did They Invent It?

Before the CSIRO's fast WLAN technology, it was very difficult to use radio waves to exchange large amounts of data quickly in an indoor environment. Radio waves would bounce off walls in enclosed spaces, causing an echo that distorted the radio signal. The CSIRO scientists used radio astronomy to solve this problem. Their detailed knowledge of how radio waves behave and their understanding of complex mathematics helped them to develop fast wireless networking technology.

Science Awards and Rewards

In 2009, Dr John O'Sullivan (who led the CSIRO team) was presented with the Prime Minister's Award for Science. In 2012, the CSIRO team were presented with a European Inventor Award. On top of this, there has been financial reward for the CSIRO, which has received more than $A430 million from companies that use the technology.

4 Access to an Online World

Over the past ten years, millions of people have gained access to mobile computing and communication devices that can access the internet at any time and from anywhere in the world. With an increase in consumer usage, telecommunications networks around the world have updated and expanded their broadband infrastructure to provide quick and reliable service amid increased internet traffic.

PERSONAL COMPUTERS

By 1997, a total of almost half a billion personal computers had been shipped to consumers from the world's PC manufacturers. Five years later, in 2002, that number had doubled! Since then, numbers have continued to rapidly increase.

Each device connected to the internet is given a unique number, or "IP address". The first numbering system used had almost 4.3 billion possible addresses, but ran out of numbers in February 2011! A new system, using 3.4 billion billion billion billion addresses is now in use. No one knows how long that will last.

A WORLD ONLINE

Top 10 Applications for Consumers' Mobile Devices

In 2012, a US-based research company estimated the top 10 applications for which people use their mobile computer devices:

MOBILE MESSAGING
communicating via text messaging and social media

MOBILE SEARCH
internet searches for information

MOBILE BROWSING
checking emails

LOCATION-BASED SERVICES
GPS navigation

MOBILE ADVERTISING
companies advertising to consumers via their mobile devices

MOBILE MUSIC
downloading music

MOBILE PAYMENT
paying for goods and services

MOBILE MONEY TRANSFERS
banking transactions

NEAR-FIELD COMMUNICATION
using mobile technology to exchange digital data and make transactions for goods and services

MOBILE HEALTH MONITORING
using applications that measure health indicators, such as heart rate or blood pressure, and store the results

5 The Key to Creating an App

The term "app" is short for application and refers to a software program that is written for a specific purpose. Today's apps are designed to be fast and easy to use for people operating in a mobile, online world.

HOW TO CREATE, DESIGN AND BUILD AN APP

Goal

To create an informative app that people will find useful or a game app that gamers will enjoy playing.

Materials

- ✓ Paper and coloured pencils or pens
- ✓ A computer
- ✓ An app builder or coding program
- ✓ App designer or game designer
- ✓ Computer programmer
- ✓ Sound engineer (optional)
- ✓ Visual artist (optional)

ESSENTIAL JOBS

These are essential jobs, but there are many other people involved in the entire process of creating a professional and successful app.

Process

1. Brainstorm ideas and concepts alone or in a team. Choose whether to develop an informative app or a game.
2. Decide on one or two really good aspects of your app, and then think about how to design it.
3. Create a storyboard to show how the user will navigate through the app.
4. Sketch the layouts for each screen in sequence, using simple yet effective logos, letters and symbols.
5. Test the layouts with friends and family to find out if the sequences are easy to follow and whether the information app is useful or the game app enticing to play.

6. Create a prototype. You could use an app builder for this or write the code yourself. Search the internet and decide on the best app-building or code-learning resource.
7. Test the prototype with as many people as possible to find out what they like and don't like about the app.
8. Write a report about the testing responses and work out how to improve the parts that people didn't like.
9. Use an app builder or write the code to build your app based on the prototype and the changes you decided to make.
10. Consider asking an application developer company to review the potential of your app.
11. Do some research to find a company that might be interested in the app you've developed. Make an appointment.
12. Prepare and practise your presentation for an application developer company.

Result
A user-friendly, functioning app that is informative or fun!

6 A High-Speed Broadband Network Improves Access

The National Broadband Network (NBN) is a project initiated by the Australian Government to provide everyone in Australia with a higher speed broadband network to cope with the growing level of internet usage. This network will enable people to download large amounts of data several hundred times faster than on the existing system.

What Is the High Speed NBN?

At the heart of the NBN is a system of new and upgraded underground fibre-optic cables in towns and cities. In remote or inaccessible areas where it is not practical or cost-effective to lay fibre-optic cables, the NBN uses fixed wireless and satellite technologies.

The NBN aims to provide about 13 million homes and businesses throughout Australia with access to high-speed internet by the early 2020s. The NBN has been installed and trialled in diverse environments around the country, such as a primary school in Tasmania, residential homes in Brunswick, Melbourne, and, in far north Queensland, the home of a family that needs online medical support for a hearing-impaired child.

An $A36 Billion Dollar Project

The NBN is a costly project because Australia is a vast country with a relatively small population compared to other developed nations. In terms of land area, Australia is roughly equal to the USA, yet its population is about 7.5 per cent of the total number of people living in the USA. This disparity means there are fewer tax-paying residents in Australia to help pay for the construction of a communications project of this magnitude.

What Are the Benefits for Individuals?

The NBN has the potential to make the daily lives of many people around Australia much easier.

Higher Speed

People can download and upload large amounts of data efficiently.

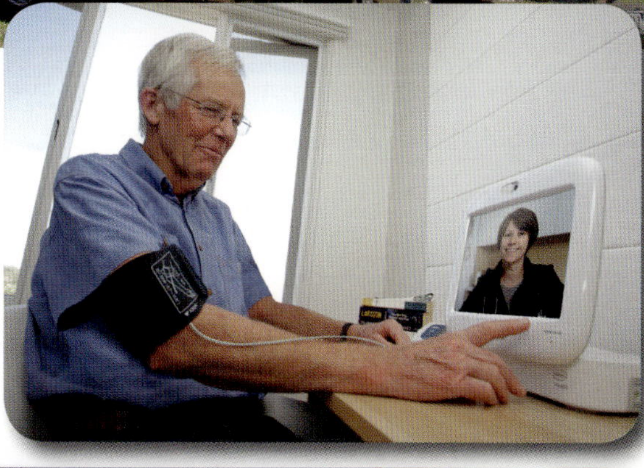

Healthcare Services

Healthcare professionals can use advanced technology to diagnose illnesses and monitor the health of patients remotely. This service gives a sense of comfort and security to patients in isolated areas and reduces the number of personal visits to overcrowded hospitals and medical clinics.

Education

Real-time online education services assist all students, especially those who live in remote areas.

What Are the Benefits for Business?

The NBN has the potential to enable businesses and their employees flexible working arrangements around Australia.

Business Opportunities

Greater network capability provides businesses with a more reliable and efficient internet service for teleconference calls and online trade with people around the country and overseas.

Teleworking

Employees can access company file sharing websites while working from home or other offsite locations. The ability of employees to telework may reduce staff turnover and absenteeism, which can occur when people are limited to working in a particular place.

How Is the NBN Installed?

Before a home is connected to the NBN, an NBN installer runs a fibre-optic cable (less than the width of a strand of hair) from the street to a small box affixed to the outside of the premises – the Premises Connection Device.

The installer drills a tiny hole through the wall in order to feed the cable through to a wall plate inside the house.

The cable is then connected to the Network Termination Device, which has a similar design to an internet modem.

In cases of power failure, an optional separate power supply box can be installed with battery backup to keep phone services operating for up to five hours.

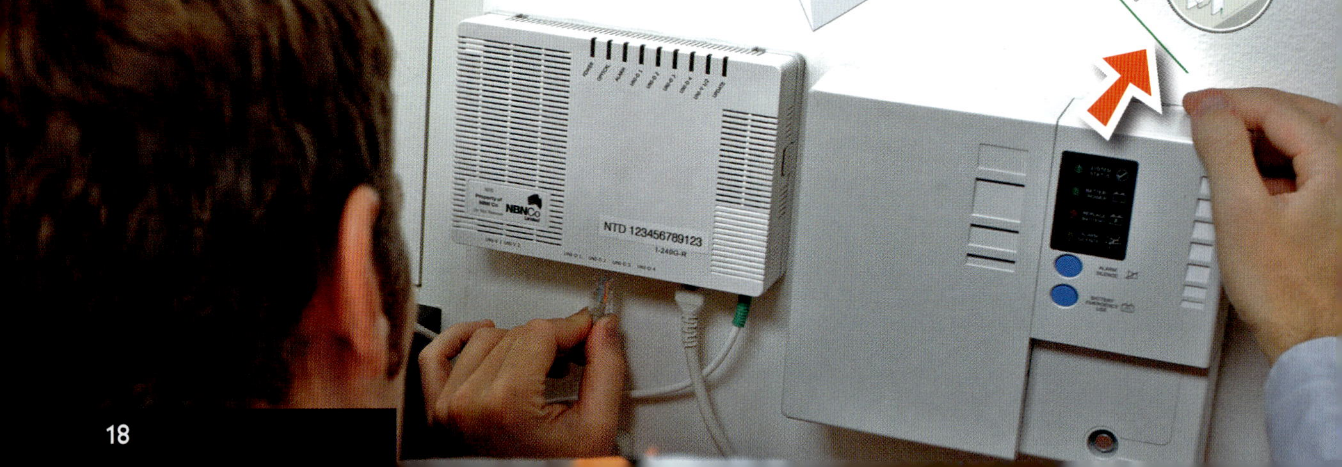

Access Technology: Key Card and Wireless

Electronic Key Card Badges

Key card access technology provides excellent security for companies and their employees, especially in places where large numbers of people work, such as shopping centres, hospitals, government buildings and space agencies. Personalised security pass badges ensure a higher level of security and access control within the organisation premises as well as privacy for individuals. This technology has many advantages for large organisations.

1. The identity of employees and visitors can be verified before granting access.
2. Authorised people have access control throughout the building.
3. Visitors can be identified and tracked efficiently; if a visitor doesn't return their access badge, the pass code in the badge will expire and prevent unauthorised entry at another time.
4. A database of people who are in the building at any time is maintained electronically.

Wireless Access

A centralised wireless security system can provide online, real-time access control for people entering and leaving a building or compound. A battery-powered wireless system uses radio frequency identification technology that can be linked to a centralised computer.

Wireless access allows real-time control of any door in the building. A wireless security system can identify door intrusion, i.e. if someone tries to enter the building without an authorised access card.

The system manager can remotely open any door from the centralised computer in times of emergency when people must evacuate the building quickly. The system will deny access to valid cards that were reported lost or stolen.

7 Electronic Access at ATMs

Most people today enjoy the convenience of automatic teller machines (ATMs) – but who first invented these machines, of which there are now over two million worldwide?

Luther George Simjian (1905–1997), an American-Armenian inventor born in Turkey, first designed and built an early version of an ATM in the late 1930s. Simjian's bank machine was trialled, but banks reported that there was little demand for it from customers, so the idea was abandoned until much later.

As with many modern inventions, there was no individual inventor of the ATM, but two British engineers are generally credited for the development of this technology.

ATM INVENTOR 1: John Shepherd-Barron (1925–2010)

John Shepherd-Barron is credited with inventing the first working cash machine. He was born in India to Scottish parents, and lived in the UK. At the time the ATM was developed, he worked for a company that printed and provided banknotes for many currencies worldwide. Shepherd-Barron's ATM invention worked with cheques, not key cards, and was first installed by the UK's Barclays Bank in 1967.

In those days, plastic key cards had not been invented. Cheques were impregnated with a mildly radioactive chemical. This encoded a four-digit personal identification number (PIN) that the user had to key into the ATM. The ATM would then dispense £10 (equal to about AU$25 today). This was the only amount a customer could withdraw.

Shepherd-Barron is quoted as saying, "I thought of the chocolate vending machine where money was put in a slot and a bar dispatched. Surely money could be dispensed in the same way."

the London location of the first ATM machine, installed in 1967

ATM INVENTOR 2: James Goodfellow (1937–)

In 1965, banks were under pressure to provide services for customers who were at work during the hours when the banks were open. English engineer James Goodfellow was asked to invent a secure system for customers to use automated cash-dispensing machines. His invention was patented in 1966, but his ATM machine was not tested until after Shepherd-Barron's ATM was installed in 1967.

Goodfellow's Challenge: Design a system that allowed only genuine bank customers to activate an ATM to withdraw cash.

Result: Goodfellow's ATM system required bank customers to use two forms of identification before the machine could be activated to issue cash.

Goodfellow's Quote: Goodfellow is quoted as saying, "I designed a system which accepted a machine readable encrypted card, to which I added a numerical keypad into which an obscurely related Personal Identification Number had to be entered manually, by the customer. This PIN was known only to the person to whom the card was issued. When these two inputs were decoded, their correspondence was checked by the system. If card and keypad inputs agreed, the cash dispenser mechanism was activated and the appropriate money was fed out to the customer."

PIN SECURITY: In the early days of Goodfellow's ATM machine, banks were concerned about this kind of electronic transaction and wanted to retain each customer's card after every transaction as a record of the cash issued. Goodfellow and his team understood that customers wanted to get their cards back, so they re-programmed the ATMs to give customers three opportunities to enter their PIN correctly before the bank retained the card.

8 Electronic Ticketing Access

On **Public** Transport

In the state of Victoria, Australia, a new electronic ticketing system called myki was introduced in 2009. The myki system uses smartcard technology to enable public transport passengers to re-use a credit-card-sized ticket that has a microchip embedded in it. The microprocessor in the card enables it to communicate with card-reader devices at train stations, in shops and on public transport vehicles. The card-reader devices communicate to a centralised system that automatically deducts fare charges or adds credit when money is deposited on to the myki card.

In Victoria, this new system provides easy access for about 410 million journeys annually across the state's network of railway stations, trams and buses.

AN ELECTRONIC PUBLIC TRANSPORT TICKETING SYSTEM

Electronic ticketing has three important advantages.

Cheapest Fares: The myki system automatically calculates the cheapest available fare.

Reusable Tickets: Unlike the previous paper tickets, the plastic card is durable enough to last for about four years.

Fare Use: By analysing electronic usage records, the Victorian government will be able to identify high-usage areas when planning new public transport services.

a Melbourne tram

On **Public** Roads

In many countries, motor vehicles are fitted with electronic tags that are used when people travel along toll roads. These devices are often called e-tags and are usually affixed to the top of the inside surface of the windscreen. How do they work?

As a motor vehicle approaches a toll gantry (a wide-span, overhead structure like a bridge or in a tunnel) the vehicle's e-tag transmits a signal to a computer attached to the toll gantry. It only takes a fraction of a second for the toll amount to be deducted from the driver's e-tag account. The toll amount pays for the use of the road and the vehicle-matching fee.

Vehicle-matching occurs when a motor vehicle's electronic access along toll roads is monitored through video tolling. With this technology, the motor vehicle's number plate is recorded on video and matched to the e-tag holder's account. If the vehicle is not fitted with an e-tag, the computer system can determine whether a pass matching the vehicle registration has been purchased.

a truck passes beneath an electronic toll gantry

International Airport Access

In Australia and New Zealand, SmartGate technology is installed at international airports for passengers with ePassports. These passports have a microchip embedded in the centre pages and an international ePassport symbol on the front cover. The microchip stores the information that appears on the person's printed data passport page and a digitised photograph, too.

SINCE 2005

ePassports have been issued since October 2005 in Australia and November 2005 in New Zealand.

How Does SmartGate Work?

The SmartGate electronic-access kiosks at international airports enable passengers over 16 years of age to self-process through passport control. SmartGate is a two-stage process. Once the passenger has been granted access they hand over their SmartGate ticket and incoming passenger card to a customs and border protection officer.

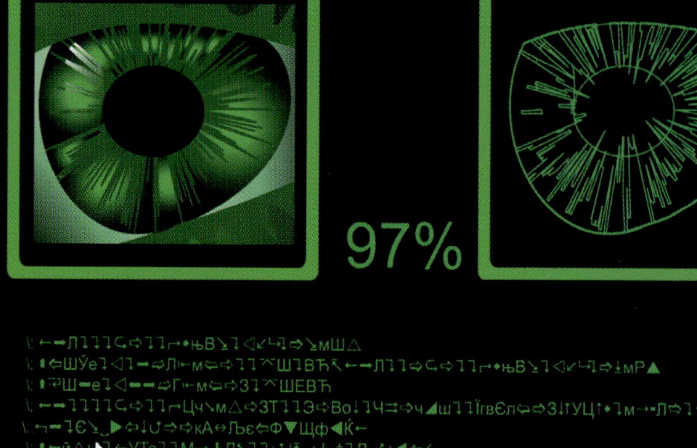

First Stage

First, the passenger places their passport into a reader at a SmartGate kiosk at passport control. The passenger is required to answer important declaration questions using the touch screen. If the questions are answered correctly, the kiosk will issue a SmartGate ticket.

Second Stage

The passenger inserts the SmartGate ticket into the gate and looks into the camera, which compares their face to their ePassport photograph. When the passenger's identity is verified, they can collect their SmartGate ticket and passport, and proceed through opened gates to baggage claim or directly to Customs and Border Protection Officers at the last checkpoint.

ACCESS GRANTED

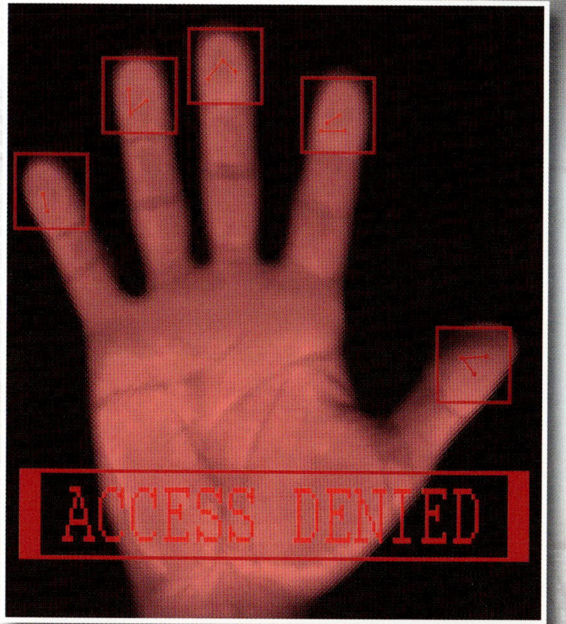

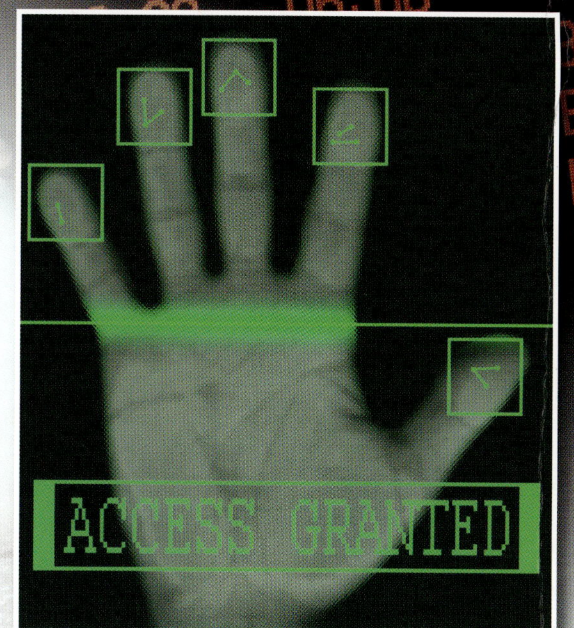

Biometrics **Technology**

Biometrics technology is designed to automatically recognise a person's physical features (e.g. iris in the eye, fingerprints) or a person's voice or behaviour. A sensor collects data such as a digital photograph of fingerprints. Then it converts the data into a format that the computer can recognise to search for person's fingerprints in a database. If there is a match, the person's identity is verified and access is granted. Biometrics technology is useful in places where many people need to be security-checked quickly and accurately, such as at international airports or government buildings.

Check-In **Technology**

Airlines offer passengers three main self-check-in options before air travel: web check-in, mobile check-in and airport-based kiosks. To create a quicker check-in experience, kiosk technology enables passengers to enter at least six different find-by options to gain access to their flight details, e.g. surname, flight number and booking reference number.

10 Electronic Access in Hotels

There once was a time when travellers were issued with metal keys to access their hotel rooms. When metal keys were lost, their replacement could be costly and inconvenient. Electronic key card technology became a viable and cost-effective alternative for accommodation providers. A key card can be produced with a magnetic strip, a smart-chip or radio frequency identification (RFID) technology.

an old-fashioned hotel key rack

RFID

Radio frequency identification is a term describing systems that transmit the identity of people or objects wirelessly using radio waves.

Most modern hotels now have key card access, because:

- **replacement costs** for lost key cards are lower
- **guest monitoring** is improved as check-in and check-out details can be coded into key cards
- **security** is improved, as only approved key card holders can access lifts and rooms.

An electronic code is put on the key card at reception (above right), which can then be used to access a hotel room (right).

How Does Room Access Technology Work?

When a guest checks in to a hotel, reception staff swipe a key card across a key card machine, which is linked to the hotel's computer, and all their information is automatically uploaded to that guest's room's key card.

Each hotel door has a battery-run microcomputer unit, which can activate an electromechanical deadbolt mechanism to open the door when the guest's coded key card is inserted into a small slot in the unit.

In addition to allowing access to hotel guests, the microcomputer can be programmed to give different levels of admission to other people, such as hotel cleaning and maintenance staff and emergency services. The microcomputer is also capable of recording the identity of all hotel personnel that gain access to a room and the time they were there.

A further feature of the microcomputer is that it will not respond to key cards encrypted with codes for previous guests, because each card covers the duration of each guest's stay.

Each key card is specific to each guest and their room.

11 Electronic Access to Computer Games

Hundreds of thousands of people around the world, many of them avid game players, work in the game development industry. It is estimated that global sales of computer games are in excess of US$60 billion annually.

Game Development

A game development company comprises a team of specialist people who design, trial and produce games that people want to play. Game development companies invest a lot of funds in creating games that they think will sell well. Before a game is ready for sale and download, the company designs a marketing campaign aimed at its intended audience. In a competitive market that is regularly swamped with new games, marketing is essential to capture people's interest.

Game Developing Jobs

Game Designers

Game designers create the ideas and mechanics of a game that will produce an enticing and fun player experience.

Computer Programmers

Computer programmers write the code that enables the game to be played.

Level Designers

Level designers work out the player's experience at each level of the game.

Game Artists

Artists fill the game's visual elements with colour and texture.

Space Invaders is one of the top three most popular arcade games and people can still play this game online.

LIVES 0

Global **Game Jam** (GGJ)

In 2009, the International Game Developers' Association (IGDA) started the first Global Game Jam (GGJ). This annual event, organised by a team of volunteers, takes place at the end of January. At that time, thousands of game developers around the world pitch their creative game design skills against each other. What makes this competition so enticing? It's like one of the best time-driven games these enthusiasts could hope to "play". In 48 hours, they must create, program and produce a game that is innovative and fun to play.

Hurry up, we've only got 47 hours, 59 minutes and 45 seconds to go!

Timeframe

At each Global Game Jam site, adrenaline-fuelled teams of game developers vie for the top prize of winning the Global Game Jam. On the Friday, GGJ teams meet at their site or workroom to view a short introductory video from the IGDA that explains the 48-hour game challenge and announces the secret theme. Once the theme is known, the teams feverishly work towards creating their games until the deadline on the Sunday afternoon. Today, this is the world's largest game jam event.

Judging Global Game Jam

So, how are thousands of entries around the world judged? A team of four judges is based at each site's workroom. Each judge will have different skills and experience; ideally there will be a computer programmer, a game designer and an artist or a technical person (e.g. audio engineer, software engineer). The judges carefully observe the creative and development process of each jamming team. At the end of the competition they will play the games before deciding the ultimate winner.

12 A Job Designing Computer Games

Imagine a job where you are encouraged to play games during your workday.

That's Jennifer's job!

Jennifer Sandercock

Jennifer Sandercock is a game designer who relocated from Melbourne, Australia, to San Francisco, USA, to work for a large game development company. She has a natural talent and passion for game designing. Jennifer plays and analyses lots of games, with the ultimate aim of creating even more enjoyable games. She says, "No game is perfect so there is always room for improvement and that's what I love about my job, working out how games can be improved."

I design games for women in their 30s and 40s – who make up over half of all game players on mobile phones and the internet.

Jennifer takes a break from working for the greater part of a 48-hour period to create and produce her team's game, Soulmate, for the 2012 Global Game Jam.

How Jennifer Became a Game Designer

Like many people, Jennifer had always been interested in games but she didn't think that game designing could become a career option for her. So, she went to university and worked in various unrelated jobs, but she still had a passion for designing games. As it turns out, Jennifer's completed university courses and degrees ended up helping her in a game-designing career:

- Masters in Artificial Intelligence
- Degree in Mechanical Engineering
- Degree in Computer Science

Jennifer's First Goals

Jennifer created a website to showcase all her games and for a year she set herself a goal to design one game each week. Jennifer first makes a prototype of each game using card or paper. By doing so, she can establish whether the game is fun to play, and if the rules of play and their sequencing work in practice. When Jennifer is confident that the game can work and is enjoyable, she builds the game on the computer.

SNOWFLAKES GAME

Jennifer explains: "The aim is to clear the snowflakes at the bottom of the screen by matching to a snowflake at the top. Matching is based on shape or colour, and the challenge occurs when players have less time to make matches. Remembering what you're matching become more challenging!"

VET GAME

Start Screen

Lucie at work

In Jennifer's own words: "Lucifer Disastrous, also known as Lucie, is an evil vet trying to live up to the expectations of her infamous father, Dr Disastrous. Unfortunately, most of Lucie's actions end up as good deeds. Join Lucie in this classic point-and-click adventure game as she explores the sides of good and evil in the small town of Darklight."

Lucie at home

Click mouse to interact with game

SOULMATE GAME

Start Screen

Jennifer also says: "My developing team and I created Soulmate for the 2012 Global Game Jam. In this game, players search for a soulmate in either of two play modes: denial and reality. In denial mode, players have as much time as they want to find a soulmate, yet in reality mode they have a limited time to find the ideal soulmate before their time runs out."

Main Game Screen

The Final Results Screen

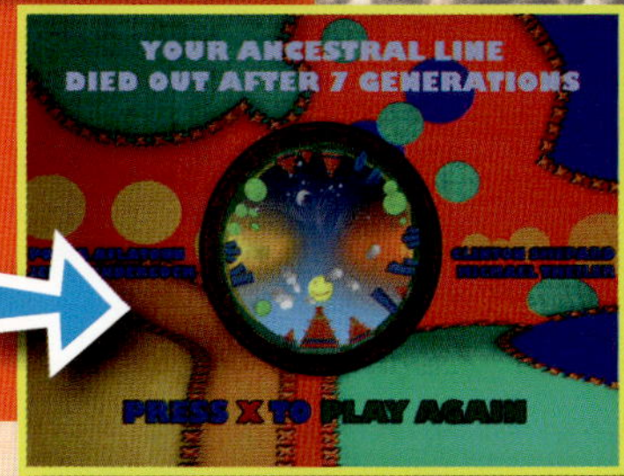

Index

Glossary

biometrics In computer science, the measurement of human characteristics to confirm identity

broadband A method of providing high-speed internet access for sending and receiving a lot of information at once

CSIRO The Commonwealth Scientific and Industrial Research Organisation is the national science research centre of Australia

GPS The Global Positioning System is a system of satellites that can provide information about your location anywhere on Earth. A GPS is also the name for a computer device that can access the Global Positioning System.

hotspot A location or place that provides internet access to the public over a wireless local area network

microprocessor A very compact unit that functions as a computer's "brain". It processes the information that is put into a computer and can be used for calculation, word processing, displaying images and video and much more.

patented When an invention has been recognised by the government as belonging to a particular inventor, so that the inventor has exclusive right to make and sell it

prototype A model or early version of something that is created to test whether an idea will work when built in its final form

radio astronomy A branch of astronomy that explores space by measuring radio frequencies that are emitted by far-off objects, such as planets and galaxies

toll road A road for which a driver must pay a fee, or toll, to drive along

verified The process of checking that someone is who they say they are or that something is what it is claimed to be